This Book Belongs to

Kalamata's Taste Bud:

Kalamata's KITCHEN

*This is for you, our readers, our next generation—our future. May your road to success be bright. Gracias a Dios por mi familia.*
—Ilma Lopez

*We would like to thank the Kalamata's Kitchen team, our families, and the incredible community of friends who have embraced this project and joined us on this adventure.*

Published by Kalamata's Kitchen
www.kalamataskitchen.com

Edited and Designed by Girl Friday Productions
www.girlfridayproductions.com

Text: Sarah Thomas
Illustration: Jo Edwards
Interior & Cover Design: Pulp + Wire and Paul Barrett

Hardcover ISBN: 9781732212602

First Edition

Printed in the United States of America

# Kalamata's Kitchen

Featuring Her Taste Buds

Al Dente and Chef Ilma Lopez

Deliciously Written by Sarah Thomas & Illustrated by Jo Edwards

# SOMETHING DELICIOUS
was happening in Kalamata's kitchen.

It was bubbling away on the stove, just out of reach. Rich, yummy smells wafting from the stewpot put her nose on high alert. She could almost taste it. Dinnertime was just around the corner, but Kalamata and her pal Al Dente were ready to dig in *now*.

Kalamata was getting hungrier by the minute. Her nose told her tummy to rumble. The simmering stew seemed to be calling to her. Mama's ticking timer was ticking away . . . *Maybe I could sneak one little bite,* she thought . . . when the doorbell rang.

Chef Ilma had come to visit! And she always brought something delicious to share.

DING DONG!

This time, Chef Ilma had brought beautiful little cakes for Kalamata. "They're topped with meringue, the way my *abuelita*, my grandma, used to make them. They're for after dinner, though."

"Thank you, Chef! But what are those?" Kalamata pointed to slices of a strange pink-and-green fruit that surrounded the fluffy cakes.

"These are guavas! We always had fruits with our cake when I was a kid. Would you like to taste one?"

Kalamata had never heard of such a funny-sounding fruit, but she was *always* excited to try a new snack.

She took a bite of the unfamiliar food. "What do you think?" asked Chef Ilma.

"I think it tastes a little like a strawberry and a little like a pear. If I got to name it, I'd call it a straw-pear-y!"

Chef Ilma looked at the burbling pot on the stove.

"What's cooking, Kalamata?" asked Chef Ilma.

"My mom calls it stew, but my tummy calls it delicious," Kalamata said. "Al Dente couldn't wait for dinner and tried to sneak a taste, but *I* told him it wouldn't be done till the *ding*!"

Chef Ilma closed her eyes and inhaled the aroma. "Mmm, with my eyes closed, I could almost be in another kitchen, far away," she said. "I wish I could show you Abuelita's kitchen. It's full of good smells. When I was little, we were always busy stirring and sifting and—"

"Tasting?" asked Kalamata hopefully.

"Yes! Tasting as you go is the only way to know!"

"I'd really like to go there with you, Chef!"

Chef Ilma smiled. "I'd like that too! But, it's very far away."

Kalamata grabbed Al and dashed under the table.

"What are you doing under there?" asked Chef Ilma quizzically.

"Come and see, Chef!"

Grown-ups didn't know, but Kalamata's table was magical. Under her table, Kalamata and Al Dente could go anywhere. The two of them had gone on many wondrous adventures together, and now, Chef Ilma was going to go too.

It was dark under the table. Chef Ilma took a big sniff. "It's strange. Something smells like Abuelita's hot chocolate . . ."

Kalamata took a big sniff too. "One time,
Al Dente went swimming in a chocolate
fountain. It was a very sticky situation," she
said solemnly.

SOMETHING DELICIOUS
was happening in Abuelita's kitchen.

"Abuelita!" cried little Ilma, surprised.

"Ilma, my *princesa*! You brought your friends. And Kalamata, I'm so happy you could join me in my kitchen. Who wants to help me cook?"

Kalamata and Ilma were ready for action.

Their first task was to crack eggs for the cake. Ilma rolled the egg on the table, then cracked the first egg.

"There's the prize!" Kalamata exclaimed, pointing at the pretty yellow blob in the bowl.

"That's the yolk!" Little Ilma laughed.

"A *yolk*, you say? Well, what's so funny about it?"

Kalamata cracked the second egg, smashing it a *bit* too hard against the table.

"Oops," she said, "I guess the *yolk* is on me now!"

"That's OK, Kalamata!" assured little Ilma. "Cracking eggs is tricky, but at least you win a prize every time!"

Abuelita showed them how to *slowly* add the flour to the mix. It slid softly into the bowl in a powdery *poof*. It was a little messy, but Al was on cleanup duty.

The cake was baking in the oven. Abuelita was at the stove, whisking hot chocolate. Good smells filled every corner of the kitchen and warmed Kalamata from her nose to her toes.

All that was left was to make the frosting for the cake. Frosting was Kalamata's favorite. Ilma picked up a whisk. "Now we'll whip up the egg whites until we have a bowl of the fluffiest cloud mountains."

They whipped . . .

. . . and they stirred.

They took turns conjuring clouds.

And soon, they had the most marvelous mountain of meringue.

They piled frosting on top of the cake. With swoops and swishes—and a few tastes, of course—they put the finishing touches on their creation.

What a masterpiece they had made! Their cake sat in the center of Abuelita's table, proudly wearing its fluffy frosting hat. Abuelita set out bowls of sweet pink guavas and cool, custardy chunks of mango and handed everyone a mug of frothy hot chocolate. Kalamata and her buds were in snack-time bliss.

Kalamata took a big breath, smelling all the good smells.
A soft ticking sound tickled her ears, and suddenly she
remembered something. She wondered if her mama's stew
was ready to eat. Just then, she heard a bright *ding!*

Kalamata loved Abuelita's kitchen, but it was time to go
back to her own.

DING

Kalamata thanked Abuelita for the wonderful adventure. She promised to bring Abuelita some of Mama's stew, and then the team hugged Abuelita goodbye.

Kalamata and Chef Ilma climbed out from under the table. There it was, that lovely smell again. Kalamata and her Taste Buds were just in time for dinner.

"Welcome back!" said Kalamata's mama, handing them each a bowl. "So, where did you go *today*?"

Kalamata and Ilma smiled at each other.

"Mama, have you ever heard of meringue?"

# RECIPES

Get going with a grown-up! You can make Abuelita's pound cake too.
Share a picture of your creation with @KalamatasKitchen on Instagram (#KalamatasKitchen).

## ABUELITA'S POUND CAKE WITH MERINGUE FROSTING, OR *MERENGADA* CAKE

1 cup (2 sticks) unsalted butter, softened
1 $1/3$ cups sugar
8 ounces cream cheese

1 teaspoon vanilla extract
6 large eggs
3 $1/2$ cups all-purpose flour
1 teaspoon baking powder

9-inch round cake pan
2 medium bowls
Electric mixer
Rubber spatula

Preheat the oven to 325° F.
Butter and flour the pan and set aside.

In one bowl, using the electric mixer, cream the butter and sugar together until the mixture is pale and fluffy. Mix in the cream cheese, vanilla, and eggs. In another bowl, sift together the flour and baking powder. Slowly add the dry flour mixture to the wet butter and cream cheese mixture and mix just until all ingredients are combined. The batter will be thick. Scrape it into the cake pan with the rubber spatula, and slide the pan into the oven. Bake for 30 to 45 minutes. After 30 minutes, insert a toothpick into the center of the cake. If the toothpick comes out clean, your cake is done! If not, bake for just a little longer. Place the pan on a rack and allow it to cool for 10 minutes. Make the meringue frosting while the cake cools. Turn the cake out onto the rack and cool completely before dolloping the meringue on the cake.

Serve immediately after frosting. Refrigerate leftovers in an airtight container. Consume the same day with lots of friends.

Enjoy!

### MERINGUE FROSTING

3 egg whites*
$1/3$ cup confectioners' sugar (adjust to taste)
$1/3$ teaspoon cream of tartar

1 medium bowl
Electric mixer or whisk

Separate the egg yolks from the whites and place the whites in the bowl. Discard the yolks (or save them for a different delicious use, like making a custard or topping a bowl of pasta!). Add the cream of tartar to the egg whites and whip until foamy. Add the sugar in batches while beating. Whip until stiff peaks have formed.

*This meringue is uncooked, so if you're concerned about eating raw eggs, consider using pasteurized egg whites. Consuming raw or undercooked eggs may increase your risk of foodborne illness.

# LEARN MORE!

**GUAVA**

A guava is a fruit that people all over the world enjoy. Guavas grow in tropical and subtropical countries, and they come in different color and flavor varieties. You can often find them in your local grocery store! Kalamata thought hers tasted like a strawberry and a pear. The next time you go to the grocery store or market, see if you can find one to taste. What do *you* think a guava tastes like? Let us know @KalamatasKitchen on Instagram (#KalamatasKitchen)!

**MERINGUE**

Meringue is a light, sweet treat made mainly from egg whites. Meringues can come in many shapes and sizes—some are soft and fluffy, like Abuelita's frosting, and some can be baked till they are chewy or crunchy. Some cooks find meringues tricky to make, but we have tips that keep it simple: Make sure the bowl is perfectly clean and dry; any residue in a bowl could prevent the meringue from fluffing up nicely. If you break any yolk into your egg whites, use a bit of shell to scoop it out. Likewise, if any shell gets into the bowl, another piece of eggshell is the easiest tool for fishing it out.

**SIMMER**

When you want to boil something, you heat it up till it's very hot and big bubbles are rapidly forming and bursting in your pot. Sometimes, though, you need the bubbles to be gentler, so that food in the pot doesn't break up, and also because sometimes it takes time to cook something *just* right. That's when you lower the temperature a little and watch the bubbles become smaller. Simmering cooks food more gently and slowly than boiling. Tell us, can you hear the difference when your stew is boiling or simmering?

To learn more about the fun kitchen tasks Kalamata and Chef Ilma performed in this adventure, head over to our website, where Chef Ilma tells you how to cream butter and sugar, the proper way to whisk egg whites, and more! www.KalamatasKitchen.com

# ABOUT KALAMATA'S TASTE BUDS

**Chef Ilma Lopez** is a James Beard–nominated pastry chef and co-owner of Piccolo and Chaval restaurants in Portland, Maine. She grew up cooking with her *abuelita* in Venezuela and loves sharing her passion in the kitchen with her own daughter, Isabella.

**Abuelita**, which means "little grandma" in Spanish, is Chef Ilma's beloved grandmother and first teacher in the kitchen. She is still inspired to cook today, even attending culinary school so she could understand what Chef Ilma experienced! She loves baking and is so excited to share her *merengada* cake with all of Kalamata's friends.

**Sarah** is Kalamata's story-chef, and she has gone on many of her own adventures under her mother's kitchen table! Sarah grew up surrounded by wonderful cooks and tasty food and is inspired by her food memories when she writes Kalamata's stories.

**Jo** is the illustrator of Kalamata's adventures and the daughter of an amazing chef. Jo was the kid who would eat anything, and she loves sharing that sense of curiosity and joy for food with her own children, Jude and Oliver.

## ABOUT KALAMATA'S KITCHEN

At Kalamata's Kitchen we seek to create a more curious, compassionate, and courageous generation of children and grown-ups using food as a bridge to diverse experiences. We believe the opportunity for adventures with food are all around us: Supermarkets can be toy stores. Kitchens can be playgrounds. Restaurants can be theaters. And everyone is welcome at our table.